PUFFIN BOOKS

-SMITH, Dick Th
RTONSH

The Schoolmouse

Dick King-Smith served in the Grenadier Guards during the Second World War, and afterwards spent twenty years as a farmer in Gloucestershire, the county of his birth. Many of his stories are inspired by his farming experiences. Later he taught at a village primary school. His first book, *The Fox Busters*, was published in 1978. Since then he has written a great number of children's books, including *The Sheep-Pig* (winner of the Guardian Award and filmed as *Babe*), *Harry's Mad*, *Noah's Brother*, *The Hodgeheg*, *Martin's Mice*, *Ace*, *The Cuckoo Child* and *Harriet's Hare* (winner of the Children's Book Award in 1995). At the British Book Awards in 1991 he was voted Children's Author of the Year. He has three children, a large number of grandchildren and several great-grandchildren, and lives in a seventeenth-century cottage only a crow's flight from

Dick King-Smith
The Schoolmouse

Illustrated by Ann Kronheimer

PUFFIN

PUFFIN BOOKS

Published by the Penguin Group
Penguin Books Ltd, 80 Strand, London WC2R 0RL, England
Penguin Putnam Inc., 375 Hudson Street, New York, New York 10014, USA
Penguin Books Australia Ltd, 250 Camberwell Road, Camberwell, Victoria 3124, Australia
Penguin Books Canada Ltd, 10 Alcorn Avenue, Toronto, Ontario, Canada M4V 3B2
Penguin Books India (P) Ltd, 11 Community Centre, Panchsheel Park, New Delhi – 110 017, India
Penguin Books (NZ) Ltd, Cnr Rosedale and Airborne Roads, Albany, Auckland, New Zealand
Penguin Boo
Penguin

Set in 15/18.5 Perpetua

Made and printed in England by Clays Ltd, St Ives plc

British Library Cataloguing in Publication Data
A CIP catalogue record for this book is available from the British Library

ISBN-13: 978-0-14-131641-3

www.greenpenguin.co.uk

MIX
Paper from
responsible sources
FSC
www.fsc.org
FSC® C018179

Penguin Books is committed to a sustainable
future for our business, our readers and our planet.
This book is made from Forest Stewardship
Council™ certified paper.

Contents

One
In Which Flora
Makes a Start

Flora was a schoolmouse.

Everyone knows that there are housemice and fieldmice and harvest-mice, and everyone knows that mice who live inside churches are called church-mice. So it's easy to guess where Flora lived.

The school was a very old one, nearly a hundred and fifty years old, in fact, and it stood in the middle of some fields.

Forty-two children went to the school (Infants

and Juniors), and about the same number of mice (fathers, mothers and children) lived permanently in its crumbly old walls and ceilings and dark cupboards, and under its worn wooden floorboards.

But of all these schoolmice, only one grew up to become interested in learning the same lessons as the children.

That was Flora.

It was as though Flora was destined to be a very special schoolmouse, for she was born on the first day of the first term of the new school year, in a hole in the wall of the Infant classroom.

Just next to the teacher's desk there was a cupboard, let in to the old whitewashed stone wall, and just above the doors of this cupboard, there was a small space between two of the stones. High up inside the cupboard a hole had been gnawed, so that a schoolmouse could run up inside and make its way into the space between the stones. From here, if it peeped out, it would have a fine view of the classroom, including a close-up of the top of the teacher's head, a couple of feet below, as she sat at her desk.

On this particular morning, a particular schoolmouse did not peep out at the Infant classroom, for it was much too busy giving birth to ten babies, one of which was the infant Flora.

All that day the mother mouse lay in the hole in the wall and suckled her new pink naked children, until school was ended, and the children had gone home, and the cleaning ladies had tidied up, and the caretaker had locked up, and the old school was empty of all life save for the jackdaws nesting in the chimneys – and the schoolmice.

Then, at last, easing herself off her sleeping babies, the mother scuttled down into the cupboard and out between its rickety old doors that never quite shut. One jump landed her on top of the teacher's desk, and another on to her chair, down the leg of which she clambered.

In the middle of the classroom floor, she could see, was another mouse, pottering about, whiskers twitching. He was searching for any little bits of anything eatable that the children might have dropped and the cleaning ladies missed.

What a husband, thought the mother mouse, whose name was Hyacinth. Here am I, brought to bed of ten children, and he's not even been to visit me, and sharply she called out, 'Robin!'

Hyacinth's husband was an untidy fellow, whose coat always looked badly in need of grooming. He had lost a part of one ear in a fight and the end of his tail in a trap, and the other schoolmice called him 'Ragged Robin'.

Now, at Hyacinth's summons, he came hurrying towards her.

'Hyce!' he cried (for it was his habit always to address his wife thus – to rhyme with 'mice'). 'Hyce, my love! I haven't seen you all day!'

'No,' said Hyacinth shortly.

'And you seem to have grown thinner, more slender, that is,' said Robin.

'Yes,' said Hyacinth.

'Have you been on a diet?'

'No,' said Hyacinth. 'I have simply lost weight.'

'How?' said Robin.

'You had better come and see.'

Up the leg of the teacher's chair they went and on to the desk-top and up inside the cupboard to the hole in the wall.

'There!' said Hyacinth, and she could not keep a note of pride from her voice. 'All yours!'

'All mine?' said Ragged Robin, and he could not keep a note of anxiety from his voice. Did she expect him to look after this swarm of ugly little pink hairless monsters? He had never had children before. What did fathers do?

'What do I do, Hyce?' he asked nervously.

'Do?' said Hyacinth. 'You don't do anything. It is I who have to suckle them and keep them warm and keep them clean and bring them up to be good mousekins. All you need to do is admire our ten children. Are they not beautiful?'

'Without doubt,' said Robin doubtfully. 'Ten, did you say?'

'Yes, as like as peas in a pod.'

But here, though she was not to know it for quite a while, Hyacinth was wrong. Alike in looks and size the babies might be, and no one, watching them as their hair grew and their eyes opened and they began to crawl about the nest, could possibly have told one from another. Yet among them, as the weeks of term went by and they grew into active, nimble mousekins, was one, a female, who was to develop into the world's most educated schoolmouse.

That one, of course, was Flora.

Whether, in fact, Flora was more intelligent than her nine brothers and sisters, we shall never know. What is certain is that she was more inquisitive. From an early age, Flora liked to poke her nose into everything. Everything interested her, and 'why' was her favourite word. Why did they live in a school? Why was the school sometimes full of people, mostly small, and why, sometimes, empty? Why did all these small people, and some big ones, come to the school? Why did the little ones look at lots of pieces of paper all joined together, with pictures on them and strange black marks and squiggles on the white paper? Why did they hold what looked like thin pieces of wood in their fat little hands and make other black marks on other sheets of paper?

All these things Flora observed, for she alone looked outward from the hole in the wall above the teacher's desk, in the Infant classroom. Always during the school day Hyacinth and the other nine kept well back inside, out of sight, but

Flora crouched at the dark mouth of the hole, watching everything that went on with the greatest curiosity.

Whether she inherited this thirst for knowledge from her matter-of-fact mother or her somewhat scatterbrained father, we shall again never know, but it did not take her long to discover that neither of them knew the answers to all her many 'whys'. It was up to her to find out.

She began the very next morning.

One thing that Flora already knew was that at some time in each day, each child would bring with it one of those joined-together wads of paper, put it down on the desk, and open it. Then the teacher would point at the black marks on the paper, one after another, from left to right, and the child would make different noises.

Day after day, Flora peered down intently, longing to make sense of whatever was going on. But her eyes, though clearly seeing the shape of the printed words on the pages of the books, could not interpret them. And her ears, though clearly hearing the child as it read, could not understand the sounds it made.

Then at last one morning came the great breakthrough that was to make all the difference to Flora's future.

She was watching attentively as usual while a little girl stood beside the teacher with her book. She was a very little girl, just beginning to learn to read, and the book was a very simple one. On each page was a large coloured picture, and below the picture a single word.

The first picture, for example, was of a round red fruit, and below it was written

Flora had never seen an apple, so the sound the child made meant nothing to her, nor had she yet in her short life set eyes on a loaf of

or (mercifully) a

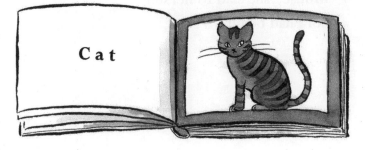

or on any of the other objects shown as the pages turned. Until the child reached M.

There was a picture that Flora immediately recognized, and below it were five little black marks on the paper, five marks like these –

Mouse

'Well?' said the teacher.

' "Mouse",' said the child, and in Flora's tiny brain something clicked. Once again she stared hungrily at those five little black marks.

'Mouse,' she said to herself.

Flora had begun to read.

Two
In Which Flora
Reads a Story

The five letters, each so different from its fellows, that made up that first word were the key to Flora's progress.

As she crouched in the hole in the wall, eagerly watching the children reading from their various books, she began to recognize those strangely shaped black marks. This was especially so when one of them was the first letter of a word that meant something to her.

The shape M, for example, stood not only for

'mouse' but for 'mother'. O was for 'owl', and though Flora had never seen one, Hyacinth had told them all what made that melancholy night-time cry outside the old school. And U began a number of common words like 'us' and 'up' and 'under', while S was for lots of things mice did, like 'squeak' and 'scurry' and 'sniff', and E for another, most important one, 'eat'.

One word led to another, and since Flora not only looked but also listened as each of the infants read to the teacher every day, she began to match the shape of the word on the page to the sound that came out of the child's mouth.

Never was there such an attentive, hard-working schoolmouse as Flora.

As Christmas approached at the end of that first term of Flora's life, something else happened which was to further her education.

One weekend, a time when the schoolmice had the place to themselves, Hyacinth called a family conference in the cupboard in the Infant classroom. Ragged Robin had taken little notice of his ten children, being too busy, like all his fellows, searching for food. But now, summoned by his wife, he gave the mousekins his full attention.

'I say, Hyce!' he cried. 'I must congratulate you, my love. You have reared ten splendid children. How strong and healthy they look.'

'They are,' said Hyacinth. 'Say hello to Daddy, children.'

'Hello, Daddy!' chorused the mousekins, all except Flora, who said, 'Hello, Father,' a word that she had recently learned.

'And now,' said Hyacinth, 'say goodbye.'

'To Daddy?' said one of the children.

'To both of us,' said Hyacinth. 'It is time you all went to seek your fortunes out in the great wide school.'

'Yippee!' cried nine of the mousekins, and away they went, out of the cupboard, on to the desk, on to the floor, and out through one or other of the doors of the Infant classroom, rejoicing that they were infants no longer.

Only Flora remained. She did not at all wish her education to be interrupted.

'Mother,' she said. 'Please can I stay here? I like it here. I wouldn't be in your way.'

'You won't,' said Hyacinth, 'because I'm not stopping. That hole in the wall is draughty. I'm off to find somewhere cosier for the next lot.'

'Next lot, Hyce?' said Robin. 'Next lot of what?'

'Babies, you booby,' said Hyacinth crossly. 'Hadn't you noticed?'

Ragged Robin looked at his wife.

'You seem to have put on weight, grown plumper, that is,' he said. 'I had not realized.'

'Hadn't you?' said Hyacinth.

'Another lot of babies,' said Robin thoughtfully. 'And so soon. I don't know how you do it, Hyce.'

Hyacinth looked at her scruffy husband with

an expression that was a mixture of scorn and resignation.

'Run along, Robin, do,' she said, 'and see if you can find somewhere really comfortable for me. Preferably not in one of the Junior classrooms – children are so noisy.'

'Right ho, Hyce,' said Ragged Robin. 'I'll try the staffroom first. Meet me there,' and off he went.

'Now, young lady,' said Hyacinth, 'just what is this all about? You saw how anxious your brothers and sisters were to be gone. Why do you want to stay here?'

'Please, Mother,' said Flora, 'it's a good place for my lessons.'

'Lessons?'

'Yes, Mother. I'm learning to read.'

'To read?' said Hyacinth. 'What on earth does that mean?'

'To make sense of the words in books, Mother. It's what the schoolchildren are taught to do. They are learning to read and so am I. It's very interesting. At first I could only read the odd word here and there, but before long I hope to be able to read a whole story.'

'Flora!' said Hyacinth sternly. 'I haven't the foggiest idea what you're talking about except that it's rubbish. Whoever heard of mice doing the same things that people do. Next thing, you'll be walking about on your hind legs. You listen to me, my girl – just forget all this nonsense. You've got too high an opinion of yourself, that's your trouble. Giving yourself airs and making out you're cleverer than the rest of us. You're just an ordinary schoolmouse and don't you forget it,' and with this Hyacinth went out through the cupboard doors and dropped carefully down to the desk and on to the floor and away.

Flora climbed up to the hole in the wall and looked out at the Infant classroom. Empty as it was, of humans and mice, there was no one to hear her say, 'I am not an ordinary schoolmouse. I'm sure I'm not. I'm sure I can learn all sorts of things that no mouse has ever learned before, if only I study hard enough, and then I shall be an extraordinary schoolmouse.'

The next day dawned. Flora never forgot that first Monday morning all on her own in the Infant classroom. Not that the other mousekins had interrupted her studies – they and their mother had mostly slept during school hours – but it was lovely to feel she had the place to herself now, ready for another happy week's work.

As if to celebrate her independence, she did something she had never before dared to do.

At midday the bell rang for lunch, and the infants lined up and then left the classroom, followed by the teacher. On her desk, by chance, a reading book had been left wide open, and Flora, seeing this, slipped down and stood before it, her little forepaws upon the edge of the page.

How big and bright the pictures were, now that she was so close, how bold and black the words!

By great good luck the book, called *Billy's Pet*, was open at page one, and when Flora had read that and page two opposite, she very much wanted to know what happened next. But, of course, there was no one to turn over the pages.

Billy, the boy in the story, wanted a pet of his own. 'But is Billy old enough,' his father asked his mother, 'to look after a pet properly?'

Is he, thought Flora? Will they let him have one? And if they do, what will it be? A rabbit? A gerbil? A guinea-pig? What colour will it be? What will it be called?

I must know, thought Flora, and carefully she poked her nose under page two and flipped it over. Once she had the knack of page-turning, keeping each flat with a foot as she read, it was easy. By the time the children came in from the playground at the end of the lunch hour, Flora was safely back in the hole in the wall. On the desk *Billy's Pet* lay open, at the last two pages now.

Flora looked down contentedly.

I must confess, she said to herself, I do like a happy ending.

Three
In Which Sweet William
Makes a Mistake

A happy ending was not in store for Flora's brothers and sisters. Unlike her, they were excitable and rather thoughtless mousekins.

Several, scavenging for food, ventured outside the walls of the school that week, never to come in again. A hungry fox, sniffing around the dustbins, snapped up one of them and the owls put paid to two more, while a fourth mousekin fell into the goldfish pond and drowned.

As for the survivors, they ran about the school

as though they owned the place, squeaking with glee at their new-found freedom.

Foolish behaviour like this was bound, sooner or later, to threaten the safety of all the other schoolmice, and, in fact, it was one of Flora's remaining brothers, a scapegrace by the name of Sweet William, who did the deed that was to lead to unhappy endings for so many.

If there's one thing that mice love, it's chocolate, and Sweet William had come upon a dusty red Smartie that some child had dropped under a desk in the Top Junior classroom.

This was the class that the Headmistress taught, and after his meal Sweet William climbed up on to her desk and began to clean his whiskers. Whether it was on account of the rich meal he had eaten or whether he did it out of bravado, we shall never know, but Sweet William positioned himself on top of the big blue class register that lay on the desk, and in the middle of it he did several rather sticky droppings.

At first, when the Top Juniors came into their

classroom next morning, no one noticed, but then a sharp-eyed boy spotted the little browny-yellow objects.

'Hey, look everybody!' he called.

'What is it?' said everybody.

The discoverer pointed proudly.

'Mouse poo,' he said, 'all over the register.'

'Ugh!' cried several, and then there was a chorus of voices.

'She'll go mad when she sees them!'

'Put them in the waste-paper bin then.'

'No, you're not allowed to touch the register.'

'Leave them, leave them, see what she says!'

'Sssh! Look out! She's coming!'

Everybody rushed to their places as the Headmistress came in and closed the classroom door. Every eye was on her. No one moved a muscle. As she sat down at the desk and put out a hand to open the register, you could have heard a pin drop. Then she saw what Sweet William had dropped.

As she looked, an expression of disgust on her

face, the tension in the Top Junior classroom was electric, and when someone giggled, it set them all off.

'Be quiet!' snapped the Headmistress, and instinctively she looked at the naughtiest boy in the class.

'Tommy,' she said, 'come here,' and when he came she pointed at the blue cardboard cover of the register and said, 'What do you know about this?'

'Please, miss,' said Tommy. 'It's mouse poo.'

'Did you put it there?'

'No, miss. I never. Honest.'

'Then who did?' said the Headmistress.

She looked round the class again and picked on the most sensible of the girls.

'Heather,' she said, 'who did this?' and Heather, sensibly, answered, 'A mouse, miss,' and the giggles broke out again.

At morning break the news flashed around the playground, and soon everyone had heard, everyone, that is, except the schoolmice. They were not to know that, thanks to Sweet William, the Headmistress was at that moment on the phone to the local authority, demanding to speak to the Pest Control Officer.

Because the old school was so small, the Headmistress's office was just a corner of the staffroom, in which at that moment there were no teachers but only, though she did not know it, eleven mice.

Ragged Robin had found Hyacinth an

excellent, snug nesting-place, under the staff-room floorboards, and in it lay Robin, Hyacinth and nine new babies, safe and comfortable and practically under the Headmistress's feet.

The two adult schoolmice listened dozily to the human voice above, but of course without understanding the significance of what was said.

'I need you to send someone out here immediately,' the Headmistress was saying. 'No, I have no idea how many mice. All I know is that there were mouse droppings on my desk this morning, and the Christmas holidays are almost upon us, and if nothing is done before the start of the next term, we shall have a plague of the creatures. What's that? You'll send a what? A Rodent Operative? When? Not until after the end of term? Why not? I see. All right. Thank you. Goodbye.'

And goodbye it would have been for every schoolmouse in the place, had it not been for Flora and her newfound skills.

On the first day of the Christmas holidays, a

man arrived at the school and was admitted by the caretaker.

'You the rat-catcher then?' he said.

'Rodent Operative,' said the Rodent Operative, a trifle huffily.

'Fuss about nothing,' said the caretaker. 'You always get a few mice in a building as old as this, right out in the fields like it is.'

'I'll soon get rid of them,' said the Rodent Operative.

'Traps, is it?' said the caretaker.

'No, no. Something tasty for the little devils to eat. That's why I didn't come earlier after it was reported. Don't want kids picking the stuff up and putting it in their mouths. You got a cat or a dog?'

'No.'

'Good. Right, I'll get on with it if you'll show me round.'

In every room of the old school, the Rodent Operative laid his baits. He opened a number of sachets and out of each sprinkled a quantity of little blue pellets on to a piece of card. When a sachet was empty, he put the polythene envelope in his pocket. By chance he came to the Infant classroom last, and because he was chatting to the caretaker for a moment before taking his leave, he forgot about the final empty sachet and left it lying on the teacher's desk. It lay there, under the gaze of two sharp eyes from the hole in the wall above.

When the men were gone and the school silent again, Flora ran down on to the desk and looked curiously, first at the piece of card on which was a cluster of strange little blue pellets, and then at the polythene sachet. There were words printed on it. Flora read them.

First, in big letters, it said

What does that mean? thought Flora, and she read on.

WARNING. KEEP MUSMORS AWAY FROM CHILDREN, AND FROM DOGS, CATS AND OTHER DOMESTIC PETS. IF TAKEN IN ERROR, CONSULT YOUR DOCTOR IMMEDIATELY.

MUSMORS IS DEATH TO ALL MICE!

Four
In Which Flora
Saves the Day

'Thank goodness I have learned to read,' said Flora, 'or else I might well have sampled these attractive-looking blue pellets.'

But then the thought occurred to her that perhaps there were other poison baits in other parts of the school that other mice might come upon. Even now her mother and father might have found a heap of Musmors. And neither of them could read!

'There is no time to be lost,' said Flora, and

she scuttled out of the Infant classroom as fast as she could go.

Never before had Flora ventured out into other places in the school, and even had she known her way about, she had no certain idea where her mother and father might be.

Then suddenly she remembered her father's words.

'I'll try the staffroom first,' he had said. That then was the most likely place to find them. But wherever was the staffroom?

Running along a passageway, Flora came to an open door and, peeping in, could see, by the number of tables and chairs and the blackboard and a teacher's desk like the one below the hole in the wall, that it was another classroom.

It was, though Flora could not know this, the Lower Junior classroom, and on one of the tables, she could see, was a mouse. It was sitting up on its hunkers, and in its paws it held something blue!

'Stop! Stop!' squeaked Flora, and running up

the leg of the table, came face to face with her brother, Sweet William.

'Hello, Flora,' he said, picking up another pellet. 'Long time no see.'

'Oh stop!' cried Flora again. 'How many of those things have you eaten?'

'Quite a lot,' said Sweet William, 'but don't worry, there are still plenty left. Help yourself.'

'No, no!' said Flora.

Oh, oh, she thought, Musmors is death to all mice. Poor Sweet William, there is nothing I can do for him now. But what about my parents? I may still be in time.

'Mother and Father,' she said. 'Where are they?'

'Haven't a clue,' said Sweet William, munching on yet another pellet. 'Matter of fact, I haven't set eyes on any of the family for yonks. Why?'

'I must find them,' said Flora.

She looked sadly at her brother.

'Goodbye,' she said softly, but Sweet William was too busy gorging himself to answer.

On the opposite side of the corridor was another classroom, that of the Top Juniors, and there Flora found a spine-chilling scene.

There were two separate heaps of blue pellets, each on its piece of card, and each surrounded by a group of schoolmice, all busy stuffing themselves with Musmors.

Hastily Flora ran round them, looking, but her mother and father were not among them. She could, though, see four more of her brothers and sisters, and to them, though she knew it was already too late, she cried, 'Don't eat that stuff!'

'Push off!' growled several older, strange

schoolmice, and one of them
made a dart at her, threatening
to bite.

Frantically Flora continued her
search and everywhere the scene was
the same. In the hall, in the library area, in
the kitchens, in every corridor and passage,
there were little heaps of the poison bait, each
with one or more schoolmice in attendance.

In one passage she found two doors. Both were
shut, but each carried a notice that she could
read. BOYS, one said and the other, GIRLS. Is
Father in one and Mother in the other, she

thought? Oh, where could they be? Would she be in time?

And then at long last she came upon a door, an open door, on which was written STAFF-ROOM. Flora dashed in. In one corner of the room was a big desk. On it was the usual card with its heap of blue pellets. And on it too was a mouse, an untidy-looking mouse with a battered ear and a tipless tail, who even at that moment was approaching the bait.

'Father!' squealed Flora in an agony of mind. 'Wait!' and she rushed across the staffroom floor and up on to the desk and put herself between Ragged Robin and certain death.

'Who are you?' said Robin.

'I'm your daughter. Flora. You know, the one that stayed behind in the hole in the wall. Oh, thank goodness I got here in time!'

'Time for what?' said Robin.

'To save your lives,' said Flora, for she could see that this pile of blue pellets was as yet untouched.

What is she talking about? thought Robin, scratching his good ear with a hind foot, and as usual when things had got too much for him, he handed the matter over to his wife.

'Hyce!' he cried, and from under the floorboards a voice replied, 'What is it?'

'Come up here,' called Robin. 'It's our Flora. She says she's come to save our lives.'

In a moment or so Hyacinth appeared at the mouth of the hole in the skirting-board and made her way up on to the desk-top.

'What's the matter?' she said grumpily. 'I've

got nine children to feed, you know, and what are you doing here, young lady, and what's all this about saving our lives, and what's that heap of blue pellets?'

'They're poison, Mother,' said Flora.

'Poison?'

'Special stuff for killing mice. My brothers and sisters have eaten it and they are going to die, and if you and Father eat it, you will both die, and then all your nine new mousekins will die, and last of all,' cried Flora dramatically, 'I shall die! Of a broken heart!'

'Pull yourself together, child,' said Hyacinth. 'How do you know this stuff kills mice?'

'I read it,' said Flora. 'On the packet. I told you, I've learned to read, just like people do. You wouldn't believe me before, but please believe me now, Mother. I don't want to be an orphan!'

Hyacinth sniffed at the blue pellets.

'They look attractive,' she said. 'Smell nice too.'

'That's just it,' said Flora. 'That's what all the

other schoolmice are saying, and soon they'll be dead! You just wait and see.'

'Load of nonsense,' said Ragged Robin. 'They look good, those things. The child doesn't know what she's talking about. Let's try some, Hyce.'

'No!' said Hyacinth sharply. 'We'll do what Flora says. We'll wait and see. We'll wait a day or so and then we'll see if one single mouse in the school has died from eating this stuff. And if by any chance it has, then I shall begin to believe in this "reading" that Flora's always on about. How long's it supposed to take this stuff to work?'

'I don't know,' Flora replied. 'It just said "quickly".'

'Load of nonsense,' said Robin again.

'We'll see,' said Hyacinth. 'In the mean time, don't you touch it. Understand?'

'Yes, Hyce,' said Robin.

'And as for you, young lady,' said Hyacinth, 'you look to me as if you could do with a good day's sleep. Off you go now, and we'll have a meeting here in the staffroom tomorrow.'

On her way back to the hole in the wall, Flora passed the open door of the Lower Junior classroom, and saw that Sweet William was no longer on the table that had held the Musmors. Nor were there any pellets left on it. He had eaten the lot.

But somewhere in the classroom someone was groaning, horribly.

Flora fled.

Five

In Which Flora
Goes Up a Class

The meeting in the staffroom next day was a grim one.

Flora had run all the way from the Infant classroom, not daring to look into either of the others as she passed. But she couldn't help noticing, as she crossed the hall, that the pieces of card there were bare of bait. It had all been eaten.

In the staffroom her worst fears were confirmed by her father. Hyacinth had sent him out on a tour of the entire school and he had not long arrived back.

'We are alone!' Flora heard him saying in funereal tones.

'No, we're not,' said Hyacinth briskly. 'Here's Flora coming.'

'That is not what I meant,' said Ragged Robin. 'We – that is, you and me and Flora and the nine mousekins – are alone in the school.'

'What?' said Hyacinth. 'Has everymouse else scarpered?'

'Everymouse else,' said Robin, 'is dead.'

There was a silence. Robin had said his piece, Flora had nothing to add, and Hyacinth was thinking.

At last she spoke.

'Flora, my girl,' she said, 'I owe you an apology. You have indeed saved our lives.'

'It's just lucky that I can read, Mother,' Flora said.

'Read something for us now,' said Hyacinth.

Flora looked around the staffroom. On one wall there was a board with a great many notices pinned on it. But it was too far from the office corner for her to read the print. However, on the wall immediately behind was a card with two large words on it, in red.

Flora pointed her muzzle at it.

'See that?' she said.

'Yes,' they answered.

'Well, that says NO SMOKING.'

'What does that mean?' they asked.

'I don't know,' said Flora. 'But I dare say I shall find out one day. There are an awful lot of things I don't know.'

'Well, I'll tell you something that *I* know, beyond the shadow of a doubt,' said Hyacinth, 'and that is that we are leaving school.'

'Leaving?' said Ragged Robin. 'Why?'

'Because,' said Hyacinth, 'the people here obviously think that the only good schoolmouse is a dead schoolmouse, and they won't rest till they've killed us too. In another few days the mousekins will be old enough to travel, and then we're off. All of us. Understood?'

'Yes,' said Robin.

'No,' said Flora.

'What was that?' said Hyacinth.

'No, Mother,' said Flora. 'I'm sorry, but I'm not coming. I've only had one term at school and I've got a great deal still to learn.'

'I'll say you have,' said Hyacinth sharply. 'I told you once before, my girl, you think too highly of yourself. You just do as I tell you.'

'No, Mother,' said Flora.

Hyacinth rounded on Robin.

'Well?' she said. 'Have you no control over the child?'

Robin looked thoughtful.

'No, Hyce,' he said.

'For the last time, Flora,' said Hyacinth, 'are you coming with us or not?'

'No,' said Flora.

'Right!' snapped Hyacinth. 'On your own head be it! I now declare this meeting closed,' and she disappeared into the hole in the skirting-board.

*

Before the Christmas holidays ended, two things had happened.

First, the Rodent Operative paid a return visit to the school.

And second, the staffroom was once more free of mice. Hyacinth, Ragged Robin and their nine new mousekins had emigrated.

'I've been picking up dead mice everywhere,' said the caretaker when he let the Rodent Operative in. 'That stuff of yours did the trick all right. They lapped it up, they did. It's all gone, barring two baits, one in the staffroom, and one in here, in the Infant classroom, which weren't touched.

'Funny,' said the Rodent Operative.

He tipped the uneaten Musmors into an envelope. Then he caught sight of the hole in the wall above the teacher's desk. He put his nose to it and sniffed.

'One in there?' said the caretaker.

The Rodent Operative nodded. He opened the cupboard doors and, looking in, saw the other entrance to Flora's hiding-place.

'Watch out inside here,' he said, and he took from his pocket a long thin gadget like a button-hook and poked it hard into the hole in the wall. But when he pulled it back out again, all it brought with it was a tangle of old nesting material. Flora had gone up a class.

Not until the caretaker had picked up the corpses, including that of poor Sweet William, had she been able to force herself to enter

the Lower
Junior classroom. But she
was determined to continue with her education,
and she reasoned that it was time for her to move
up in the school. After all, she thought, I am
older now.

It was too much to hope that there would be
another conveniently placed hole in the wall,
and, indeed, there wasn't. But Flora was in luck
nevertheless. Behind the Lower Juniors'
teacher's desk was a long bookshelf. Like all

mice, Flora could run up a sheer wall if it was roughcast and not too high, and she got up on to this shelf without much trouble.

The books on it were loosely arranged, and squeezing between two of them, Flora found that the shelf was so deep that there was plenty of room behind, room and to spare for a schoolmouse keen to continue with her studies. She would be able to run up and down behind the line of books and peep out wherever there was a space.

I'll be better off than when I was an Infant, she thought – I'll be able to look down on some of the children's tables as well as the teacher's desk. And there's a nice view of the blackboard.

Flora waited anxiously for the start of the spring term.

On the day before it began there was a staff meeting.

'One final thing,' said the Headmistress to the Infant teacher and the Lower Junior teacher and the part-timer who came in two days a week to take the Top Juniors, 'that I know you'll be glad to hear. We are all animal lovers, I'm sure, but I'm happy to tell you that the local authority sent a man during the holidays who has exterminated all the mice. There is not a mouse alive anywhere in this school, not one.'

Six
In Which Hyacinth Leads the Way

Hyacinth had not lightly made the decision to leave school. She was aware that to journey with her family to some new, as yet unknown, home would be a hazardous business.

But already she had lost nine children, her entire first litter of mousekins save for that stubborn girl Flora, and she did not want to lose another nine. For her, the school was now a place of death, and it was her duty to take them abroad, whatever the risks.

'And it is your duty to accompany us,' she said to her husband.

'But, Hyce . . .' began Ragged Robin.

'No buts,' said Hyacinth.

So it was that, some nights after the great massacre, Hyacinth led the way out of the staffroom, out of the school, across the playground, and into the fields.

Following her in single file came the nine mousekins, while a nervous Robin brought up the rear, casting fearful glances all around him as they threaded their way through the darkness.

For some reason it had tickled Hyacinth's fancy to give her second litter names beginning with the same letter, and as soon as they were clear of the school grounds she took a roll-call.

'Lily?' she called.

'Here, Mum.'

'Lilac? Lotus? Lupin?'

'Here, Mum, here, Mum, here, Mum.'

'Lobelia? Laburnum? Larkspur? Lavender?' and there was a chorus of 'Here, Mum's.

'Now who have I left out?'

'Me, Mum,' piped a little voice.

'Who are you?'

'Love-in-a-mist, Mum.'

'And me, Hyce,' said a rather hurt voice.

'Yes, yes, and you, Robin,' said Hyacinth. 'Now then, keep close together, nose to tail, and not a squeak out of any of you.' Or the owls will get you, she thought. I only hope we can find shelter before long. I can't think how fieldmice manage, living out here.

Walking across even a large field is nothing to a human being, but the mousekins soon wearied of battling their way through the long grass. Despite whispers of 'Sssh, darlings' from Hyacinth and 'Be quiet, you little fools' from their father, there was soon a chorus of unhappy cries.

'How much further?'

'Are we nearly there?'

'Can we have a rest?'

'I'm tired.'

'I'm cold.'

'I'm hungry.'

'I feel sick.'

'My feet hurt,' piped the mousekins as they struggled along, and from the smallest, Love-in-a-mist, came a final cry of, 'Mum! Stop! I can't go any further.'

Just at that moment Hyacinth saw a large squarish shape looming up in the corner of the big field.

'Come along, darlings,' she cried. 'We're nearly there,' and she ran forward, to find herself at the foot of a great stack of straw bales. At that very minute an eerie wavering call sounded from

the upper branches
of a nearby hedgerow tree.

'Tu-whit!' it said. 'Tu-whit!' and then 'Ho-hoo-hoo-hoooooo!'

'Quickly!' cried Hyacinth. 'Hurry, all of you!' and at the sound of her voice, the tawny owl launched itself from its perch.

Frantically Robin at the rear urged on his exhausted children – Lily, Lilac, Lotus, Lupin, Lobelia, Laburnum, Larkspur, Lavender and little Love-in-a-mist – and frantically the mousekins scuttled towards safety.

'In here!' cried Hyacinth, diving into a gap between two straw-bales, and in there they dashed as the owl swooped silently down, its talons spread ready to grip, its great golden eyes fixed on the last in line, Ragged Robin.

From inside the safety of the stack, Hyacinth heard him give a single piercing squeal, and then there was a horrid silence.

Hyacinth's heart missed a beat. He's been killed, she thought, my Robin's been killed, and it need never have happened. We should never have left the school. It's all my fault. I and I alone am to blame. And now I am a widow.

She gathered her mousekins about her.

'Children,' she said in tones of deepest woe, 'your father has gone.'

'Where's he gone, Mum?' said Lotus.

'West,' said Hyacinth. 'He has passed over.'

'Over what, Mum?' said Lobelia.

'Over the Great Divide,' said Hyacinth. 'He's had it.'

'Mum,' said Lupin. 'What's he had?'

'Oh, for goodness' sake!' said Hyacinth sharply. 'Daddy's dead.'

There was a moment's silence and then, in a very small voice, 'Poor Daddy,' said little Love-in-a-mist.

Suddenly Hyacinth thought she heard a distant cry. A muffled cry it was, coming from somewhere far back along the tunnels between the straw-bales through which they had come.

'Hyce!' came the muffled cry. 'Hyce! Where are you?'

Robin's ghost, said Hyacinth to herself in an agony of spirit, come to haunt me for the rest of my days.

But then the sound grew louder, and before long a familiar face appeared. An untidy sort of face it was, with one battered ear, but it was solid flesh and blood nevertheless.

'Oh, Hyce!' said Ragged Robin. 'That was a narrow squeak.'

In fact the owl's dive had been a fraction of a second too late. When it landed in a flurry of loose straw at the foot of the stack, all that was still showing of Robin was his tail, that tail that had already been shortened in an old fight, and the best that the owl could do was to chop at it as the mouse disappeared.

'Robin!' cried Hyacinth, and 'Daddy!' cried the nine mousekins.

'Oh Robin!' said Hyacinth. 'I thought I had lost you. I never was so hurt.'

'Nor I,' said Robin.

'I heard that awful squeal,' said Hyacinth, 'and I thought you had come to a sticky end.'

'I suppose I have, in a way, Hyce,' said Ragged Robin, and he turned himself around so that they could see.

All that was left of his tail was a bloodstained stump.

Seven
In Which Flora
Sees a Ghost

'There is not a mouse alive anywhere in this school, not one,' the Headmistress had said at the staff meeting. She was wrong.

What's more, on the very next day there were two.

One, of course, was Flora. The other belonged to Tommy, the naughtiest boy in the Top Junior class.

Christmas is a time when people are sometimes given unsuitable presents. Often these are pets. Everyone knows that many puppies are bought by the wrong people for the wrong reasons and soon after discarded, often cruelly.

Smaller pets can suffer the same fate, and Tommy had been given a pet mouse as a Christmas present.

For a few days it was a novelty for him, and he quite liked feeding it and watching it working away at the little treadmill that was fitted in its cage. But then he became bored with it. The pet mouse was bored too – that's why it spent its time in the treadmill – and, no doubt, in due course Tommy would have neglected it. But then he had a brilliant idea.

He remembered the disgust that the Headmistress had shown on finding mouse droppings on her register at the end of last term. And I bet she's scared stiff of mice, he thought (and the other teachers too, with a bit of luck). I'll take my mouse into school and let it go on her desk. I bet she'll have forty fits!

So it was that on the very first day of the spring term, Tommy took his mouse with him, secretly of course, for pets were not allowed in school. He brought it in a little cardboard box which he hid in the locker where he kept his books. He did not tell any of his friends.

All morning he sat imagining the scene. He would wait till after lunch, till after the midday break. Then, when they came in from the playground, he would take the mouse out of its box and let it go on the Headmistress's desk, just a moment before she entered the classroom. OK, so he'd be punished. He didn't care. It would all be worth it, just to see her face and hear her scream!

But as everyone knows, the best-laid schemes of mice and men don't always quite work out. When Tommy came in from the playground at one o'clock and hurried to open the little cardboard box, it was empty. In one side of it a mouse-sized hole had been gnawed.

All that afternoon Tommy sat, hopefully waiting, his eyes darting about the Top Junior classroom. The mouse must be somewhere around. Things might still work out all right, if only he could spot it and catch it, at afternoon break perhaps. But there was no sign of it.

Maybe it'll turn up tomorrow, Tommy said to himself, and if it doesn't, what do I care? I'm tired of the stupid thing anyway.

Neither on the next day nor on those that

followed was there any sign of Tommy's mouse. Meanwhile Flora was getting into the swing of the spring term. The bookshelf was proving to be a great success, both as a home and as a vantage point. By peeping out at various spots between the loosely stacked books, Flora the Lower Junior could see much more than had Flora the Infant, stuck in the hole in the wall.

Now, as well as surveying the teacher's desk, she could also see what a number of children were doing at their work-tables. There were more snatches of new books for her to read, and by watching carefully during maths lessons, Flora came gradually to understand the symbols that stood for different numbers. Also there was a large calendar on the opposite wall, with the dates in very big red figures, and by studying these, Flora learned to count. But not, of course, beyond 31.

While the children were in school, Flora was as happy as could be, busy with her lessons. And at playtime or during the lunch hour, when the classroom was empty, she would leave the bookshelf and scuttle about, climbing on to the tables and studying any book that had been left open. In this way she learned a number of things not normally known to mice.

For example, she read that the earth went round the sun, that David slew Goliath, that Paris was the capital of France,

and that Henry VIII had six wives. She did not understand the full meaning of these interesting facts, but she stored them away in her memory in case they should come in useful one day.

Food, now that she was the only schoolmouse in the place, was much easier to come by. She soon learned the order in which the cleaning ladies did the hall and the various classrooms after school, and she usually contrived to nip round ahead of them, picking up the crumbs and bits of food that the children had dropped.

It was only when the school was empty of people and night fell that Flora was less than comfortable. Partly, she was lonely. She had always been independent by nature, but she found herself missing her parents and wondering about the nine new mousekins she had never as yet set eyes on. Where were they all now?

Partly, she was afraid, as she thought about her own nine brothers and sisters, all dead and gone, and particularly of Sweet William who had died in the very classroom in which she now lived.

One stormy night of thunder and lightning, when the wind was howling around the old school, Flora sat remembering his horrible groans. What if the ghost of Sweet William should appear to me, she thought? She peered out between her books and, as she did so, a flash of lightning lit up, just for a second, the Lower Junior classroom. But in that second Flora saw clearly the figure that even now was crossing the floor towards her.

It was the figure of a mouse, a mouse whose eyes shone blood-red in the glare of light, a mouse whose coat was not the grey-brown of other, ordinary mice, but a pure ghastly ghostly white!

Eight
In Which Buck Moves In

Flora let out a squeal of terror.

'Keep away from me, Sweet William, keep away!' she squeaked, and a grumpy voice answered, 'Who are you calling Sweet William?'

Do ghosts talk, thought Flora?

'Are you a real mouse?' she said.

'Of course I am,' said the grumpy voice.

'But you're white.'

'So what? Lots of pet mice are white.'

'Oh,' said Flora. 'I didn't know.'

'I dare say there are a lot of things you don't know,' said the white mouse.

Flora was rather hurt at this. I bet I know more than he does, she thought, for her nose now told her she was addressing a male. She remembered something she had learned that very afternoon.

'I know the name of the mother of the Queen,' she said. 'Do you?'

'No,' said the white mouse. 'What is it?'

'The Queen Mother.'

The white mouse made no reply to this piece of information. Another lightning flash showed Flora that he had turned his back on her and was sitting up and cleaning his whiskers.

He is rather rude, Flora thought.

After a while he said, 'Well, what's your name?'

'Flora. What's yours?'

'Mother always called me "Buck",' said the white mouse.

'Buck', thought Flora. That's silly. That's like a pig calling her son 'Boar', or a cow calling hers 'Bull'.

'Why?' she said.

'Because I was the only boy among six of us. She gave my five sisters pretty names, but she just called me "Buck", and Buck has stuck, worse luck.'

He doesn't sound very happy, Flora thought. She ran down the wall beneath the bookshelf and approached the stranger.

'You don't sound very happy,' she said.

'I'm not,' said Buck, 'and nor would you be in my place. A couple of weeks ago I was living comfortably in a pet shop, warm and clean and well fed. And then I was picked out – held up by my tail, I'll have you know – and given to a stupid boy. I could tell by the way he handled me that he knew nothing about animals, and then, to cap it all, he put me in a box and brought me to this place.'

'And you escaped?' said Flora.

'Yes, and I've been trying to keep out of sight since. At least I'm free. The last thing I want is for that stupid boy to find me again. By the way, you're the first mouse I've met here.'

'I'm the only mouse in the school,' said Flora.

'So this is a school, is it?' said Buck.

'Yes,' said Flora. 'It's a place where they teach young human beings to read and write and do sums and stuff like that.'

'Reading? Writing? Sums? Don't know what you mean,' said Buck. 'But it explains why there are so many of the noisy creatures about. It's a wonder that none of them have spotted me yet.'

Especially as you're white, Flora thought.

The storm had moved away while they were talking, the thunder distant now, and the wind's howl had dropped to a mere humming. Through the tall windows of the Lower Junior classroom came the first light of dawn, and Buck ceased his grooming and turned his pink eyes on Flora.

'That's better,' he said. 'Now I can see you properly. My night sight is very poor, I'm afraid – it's the same with all us pink-eyed whites, you know. We're none of us blessed with good vision.'

Flora, whose sight was excellent by day or night, immediately felt sorry for him. And that was not all she felt. How handsome he is, she thought, so large and sleek. And those wonderful red eyes – they make me go quite weak at the knees. And that gleaming coat of his, white as the driven snow – how beautiful it is. And how dangerous! It can only be a matter of time before he will be recaptured, she said to herself, so conspicuous is he. And then I shall lose him. And I don't want to.

While she was thinking all these thoughts, Buck continued to stare at her without speaking. Then he said, 'Why do you live by yourself in the school?'

'I'm a schoolmouse,' Flora said.

'Yes, but why are you alone?' said Buck. 'I mean, I should have thought you'd have had lots of admirers, pretty girl like you.'

'No,' said Flora.

'Oh,' said Buck.

There was quite a long silence as the two so different-looking mice crouched on the classroom floor, in broad daylight now.

At last Flora spoke.

'Buck,' she said.

'Yes?'

'I may call you Buck?'

'Of course, Flora.'

'Are you planning to stay here, in the school?'

'Certainly I am,' said Buck. 'You, who have

been free all your life, to go where you
like and do what you please, can't
imagine the joy of freedom to someone
like me. My life so far has been one of
imprisonment, but no longer.'

'Then we must make plans,' said Flora.
'People will be coming into the school before
long, and they mustn't see you.'

Then she had a thought. Recently she had
come upon a natural history book open at a page

about camouflage. She did not quite know how to pronounce the word, but she could see what it meant from the pictures. One was of a tiger, its striped coat blending into the jungle background, and one of a drab-coloured bird, almost invisible on its nest among a tangle of grasses.

'If you were to get your coat really dirty,' she said, 'you wouldn't be nearly as noticeable.'

'No,' said Buck. 'No, Flora, I'm sorry, but I draw the line at that. I have always prided myself on being well turned out. The slightest speck of dirt on my coat upsets me no end. I can't bear a scruffy mouse.'

You wouldn't think much of Father then, thought Flora, as she watched Buck fall once more to grooming himself.

'You'll have to be hidden then,' she said, 'for the whole of the school day. We must find somewhere safe, and quickly too. Let me think.'

He must go underground, she thought, under the floorboards somewhere, as Mother and Father did in the staffroom. There, perhaps? No, it was too far away, she must have him close. Surely there must be somewhere in this very classroom.

Flora began to run about, searching, and almost at once luck was with her. In one corner of the Lower Junior classroom stood a sink, where the children washed up their brushes and pots after painting lessons. A hole had been cut in the floor to take the drainpipe that ran down from this sink, and around the edge of this hole there was ample room for a mouse to get down.

Flora got down, and found that there was a comfortable space beneath, where Buck might be undisturbed save for the occasional gurgle of running water.

'Quick!' she called. 'Down here, Buck.'

'Now,' she said when he had found her, 'you'll just have to stay here all day and not make a sound. Have a good sleep, I should. I'll come and fetch you at the end of school.'

'But, Flora,' said Buck. 'Aren't you going to stay here with me?'

'No,' said Flora. 'You must remember, Buck, that I am a schoolmouse. I have an awful lot to learn.'

'I don't quite understand,' said Buck.

There was a distant noise as the front door of the school was unlocked.

'I can't explain now,' said Flora hurriedly. 'I've got to go or I shall miss my lessons.'

Buck's eyes glowed red in the darkness under the floorboards.

'I shall miss you,' he said softly.

Nine
In Which Robin Obeys Orders

Meanwhile back at the stack, the schoolmouse family had settled in. There was plenty of food, for in the straw were a great many grains of barley that the combine harvester had missed, and there was warmth and shelter among the bales. There was no shortage of comfort, but there was also no shortage of enemies.

Ragged Robin's wound had healed pretty well, but each night the cry of the tawny owl reminded him of his narrow escape. Other visitors to the stack included foxes and an old tomcat living wild.

'Just stay inside,' said Hyacinth to the mousekins, 'and you'll be safe from cat, fox or owl. They cannot get in among the bales.'

But someone else could.

One night a week or so after the meeting of Flora and Buck, the straw stack was as usual a hive of activity. At the cold end of January, it was home to a wide variety of rodents, and in the dozens of runways between the bales lived rats, and voles, fieldmice, harvest-mice, and shrews, together with a good many ordinary housemice, and not forgetting the eleven schoolmice.

The tawny owl, looking down from its perch in an oak tree, saw a little animal at the base of the stack, scampering along the ground straight-bodied as though it had no legs. In colour it was a reddish brown with a white underside, and it was no more than eight inches in length. For an instant it paused at an entrance hole between two bales, one forefoot lifted, its short tail erect.

Then, even as the owl launched itself, the weasel disappeared into the stack.

The owl circled and flew up again on to its perch and stood with its back against the trunk of the oak, listening. So sharp was its hearing that it clearly heard the sudden panic-stricken scurrying and scuttling within, and then a single terrified squeak that died abruptly away.

Hyacinth heard it too from the nesting-place she had chosen deep inside the stack. Hastily she called the mousekins to her and took a roll-call. All answered to their names but one. Laburnum was absent.

Just then Ragged Robin appeared, his eyes nearly popping out of his head.

'Oh, Hyce!' he cried. 'It nearly got me!'

'What nearly got you?' said Hyacinth.

'Oh, it was horrible!' said Robin. 'I saw it go by and it looked awful and it smelt awful and it was making a horrid hissing noise and I came across an old rat and I said, "What is it?" and he said, "Weasel", and his teeth were chattering and his hair was standing on end and he was shaking with fright even though he must have been five times the size of the thing and then it must have killed a mouse. I heard it squeak.'

'Laburnum,' said Hyacinth.

'But, Mum,' cried the eight remaining mousekins, 'you said we'd be safe inside the stack, you said nothing could get in, that's what you said.'

Before Hyacinth could answer, they all heard the horrid hissing noise of which Robin had spoken, and in a blind panic the schoolmouse family fled in every direction.

For the blood-thirsty weasel it was a red-letter night. It snaked its way through the straw labyrinth, killing for the sake of killing, and Hyacinth's mousekins in particular were easy prey.

By the end of the night it had put paid to three more of them.

From then on, things went from bad to worse. Fear that the weasel might return led the survivors to risk a search for hiding-places outside the straw stack, and, as time went by, owl, cat and fox accounted for four more. Until by the end of March the only survivors of the family of schoolmice were Hyacinth, Ragged Robin and one remaining daughter, little Love-in-a-mist, who had stuck close to her mother throughout.

'Nineteen children I have born,' said Hyacinth, 'and only this poor mite to show for it.'

'You're forgetting, Hyce,' said Robin. 'There's Flora.'

'Oh yes. That stubborn girl.'

'I wonder how she's getting on,' said Robin.

Hyacinth looked thoughtfully at her mate.

'I think we should find out,' she said.

'Find out?' said Robin. 'How can we find out? She is in the school. We are in the stack.'

'Not for much longer, I hope,' said Hyacinth. 'It's a death-trap.'

Ragged Robin looked smugly at his wife.

'It was you that brought us here, Hyce,' he said.

Hyacinth looked angrily at her scruffy, dog-eared, tail-less husband.

'That's right, blame me for everything,' she said.

'Mum,' said Love-in-a-mist. 'Why did we leave school?'

'It wasn't safe there,' said Hyacinth. 'There was poison.'

'While out here,' said Robin tartly, 'we've only got owls and cats and foxes and weasels to worry about.'

'All right, all right,' snapped Hyacinth. 'We will go back. Providing Flora has survived. Go on, go and find out.'

'Who, me?' said Robin.

'Well, you don't think I meant Love-in-a-mist, do you?'

'It's quite a step,' said Robin. 'Right across the other side of that great field, a long way for an old chap like me, but no distance for her young legs. And she's got a tail, what's more.'

'Love-in-a-mist,' said Hyacinth. 'Run away and play. I wish to speak seriously to your father.'

So it was that some hours later a tail-less mouse was to be seen making his nervous way over the field, across the playground, and towards the school buildings. Ragged Robin was heading for the Infant classroom where he thought to find Flora, when suddenly a voice behind him said, 'Hey, you!'

Robin turned to find himself facing a strange mouse, a mouse a good bit larger than himself, a mouse, what's more, with pink eyes and a coat of gleaming white, who was marching purposefully towards him.

'Hey, you!' said the white mouse again.

'Who, me?' said Robin.

'Yes, you, you shabby old bobtailed has-been. What do you want?'

'I want to see Flora.'

'Not on your life!' cried the white mouse, and with a squeak of anger, he threw himself upon the unfortunate Robin.

Ten

In Which Robin
Comes Off Worst

In his younger days Ragged Robin had been a strong fighter, but those times were long past. Youth and the advantage of weight were on Buck's side, as was the element of surprise in the attack, and Robin fared badly. He was specially handicapped by the lack of a tail, so important to a mouse's balance, and he gave ground in the face of his attacker's fury.

'Want to see Flora, do you?' growled Buck. 'She's my Flora, understand? Mine!'

'But she's my Flora!' panted Robin, and then he let out a squeal of pain as the white mouse bit him through the foot.

The noise of the scuffle brought Flora rushing to the scene, a scene that filled her with horror. Outclassed by his young strong opponent, Robin was indeed ragged. Battered and blood-flecked, he still fought on desperately on three legs, but the outcome of the battle was obvious.

Flora thrust herself between the combatants.

'Stop, Buck! Stop!' she cried. 'Don't you know what you're doing?'

'Yes,' said Buck. 'I'm beating up this intruder, nasty scruffy old thing. What's more, he's gone and bled all over my clean coat. Said he wanted to see you. What's he want with a young girl like you – he's just a dirty old mouse.'

'He's not!' said Flora. 'He's my father!'

'Your father?' said Buck in astonishment.

'Yes, and you've hurt his poor foot. And you call yourself my boyfriend.'

'Your boyfriend?' said Robin in amazement.

'And oh, oh,' Flora went on, 'you've bitten his tail off!'

'I didn't,' said Buck. 'Did I?'

'No, Flora,' said Robin. 'He didn't do that. But it's a good job you turned up or he'd have made an end of me.'

'Oh, Father!' cried Flora. 'Will you be all right? And where's Mother? And where are the mousekins? And why are you here?'

'I came to see you, Flora,' said Robin. 'Like I told what's-his-name here.'

'Buck,' said Flora. 'He's called Buck. And he's got something to say to you.'

Buck looked up from cleaning the spots of blood off his coat.

'I have?' he said.

'Yes,' said Flora, and there was an echo of her mother in the tone of her voice and the set of her jaw. 'You are going to say you are sorry.'

'Shan't,' said Buck.

'Very well,' said Flora. 'In that case, I shall never squeak to you again,' and she marched off.

'High-spirited girl,' said Robin, licking his wounded foot. 'Takes after her mother.'

Buck looked curiously at this old wreck of a mouse. Flora's dad, he thought, who'd have guessed, when she's so neat and pretty. And angry, he said to himself. Maybe I'd better try to put things right, though I can't see there's any need to apologize. He should have said who he was in the first place. He cleared his throat.

'You put up a pretty good scrap,' he said. 'For an old 'un, that is.'

'I've won a few fights in my time,' said Robin.

There was a silence, while Buck cast about for something to say.

'Foot hurt?' he asked at last.

'Yes,' said Robin.

'Ah,' said Buck.

Another silence ensued. It was light by now, but there was no need for concealment. It was the Easter holidays, and the school was empty.

'If you don't mind me asking,' said Buck, at length, 'how did you lose your tail?'

'Owl,' said Robin.

'Oh,' said Buck.

He's not very talkative, he thought. What can I say to please the old devil? Oh yes, I know.

'Your daughter Flora,' he said. 'Prettiest girl I've ever seen.'

Robin stopped his licking and looked up into the pink eyes.

'Spitting image of her mother,' he said.

'Really?'

'Yes. Hyacinth is a great beauty.'

'Hyacinth. That's a nice name. By the way, I don't know yours.'

'Robin.'

'Robin,' said Buck. 'That's a nice name too.'

'You think so?'

'Definitely. And Flora, of course, is a lovely name.'

'Keen on her, are you?'

'I certainly am, Robin,' said Buck.

'And she's . . . um . . . fond of you?'

'Yes, I'm a lucky fellow.'

You're a handsome fellow, thought Robin, with those pink eyes and that snow-white coat. Not surprised she's fallen for you.

'I never could understand,' he said, 'why Hyacinth picked me. I wasn't the best-looking of mice then, and I'm certainly not now.'

Poor old chap, thought Buck, with his busted ear and no tail and now I've gone and lamed him. Not surprised Flora blew her top.

'I'm sorry,' he said.

'What's that?' said Robin.

'I'm sorry I knocked you about, Robin.'

'Oh,' said Robin. 'Oh, that's all right. Decent of you to say so, er, Buck.'

Flora had heard every word of this conversation. After she had flounced out, she hid and listened, and on hearing Buck's apology, she came running back.

'Now, Father,' she said, 'tell me. How is everybody? And what are you doing here?'

So Robin related all that had happened since

leaving school,
while Flora listened
with little cries of 'Oh,
no!' and Buck's pink eyes
bulged with horror at this tale
of death and disaster.

'So I came back to see how things were here,' finished Robin. 'Or rather your mother sent me. Which reminds me, I must report back to her at the straw stack. She'll be wondering what's happened to me, she and little Love-in-a-mist. That is, if something awful hasn't already happened to them. I must go straight away.'

'You cannot, Father,' said Flora. 'You can't even put that foot to the ground, let alone travel all that way back.'

'But someone must fetch them,' said Robin.

'Let me,' said Buck.

'Good of you to offer, my boy,' said Robin, 'but it would be suicide for a mouse of your colour. No, no, I must go.'

'You will do nothing of the sort,' said Flora.

'But, Flora,' said her father, 'we cannot simply leave them there, in that death-trap.'

'No,' said Flora. 'I shall go and fetch them.'

Eleven
In Which Flora
Takes a Journey

Before the others could open their mouths to protest, Flora was gone. Her father, she knew, could not follow her, and Buck, she hoped, would not. What with his poor sight and sense of smell much less sharp than that of a wild mouse, she shuddered to think what might befall him out in the open in broad daylight. Or what might befall me for that matter, she said to herself. Nevertheless she pressed bravely on, hoping to sight the straw stack before too long.

In fact, she could hardly see beyond the end of her nose, so much had the spring grass grown. What she could do though was to hear something. At first it was just a distant rumble, but quickly it grew louder, until it became a roaring, thundering, deafening noise heading straight for her, while the ground beneath her feet shook.

Flora cast a terrified glance behind her, to see a huge red monster approaching. Leaping madly away to get out of its path, she came to a bank at the field's edge, a bank in which, she saw, there was a large hole. Flora dived headlong into the hole as the monster went lumbering by.

For a long while she crouched there, too

frightened to move. Then at last she heard
something approaching her from the inside of
the burrow in whose mouth she sat, and before
she could decide what to do, a large animal
appeared. It was large, that is to say, to Flora's
eyes, and brown in colour, with a furry coat and
big liquid eyes and long ears that stuck up.

'What's up then, mouse?' said the animal. It
had two large front teeth, Flora could see, but
something told her that it was not dangerous,
and she held her ground.

'Sorry to intrude,' she said, 'but I was being chased by a red monster.'

'Red monster!' said the animal. 'What be you then — some kind of town mouse?'

'No,' said Flora. 'I'm a schoolmouse. And please, what are you?'

'You don't know?'

'No.'

'Where you been all your life, mouse?'

'In school.'

'You ain't learned much then. Never seen a rabbit before?'

thought Flora. Of course! I remember seeing a picture in that very first book I ever looked at.

'Only in a book,' she said.

The rabbit shook his long ears in bewilderment.

'You soft in the head, mouse?' he said. 'All this yer stuff about schoolmice and books and red monsters: anyone'd think you ain't never seen a tractor before neither.'

thought Flora. Yes, that was in the book too.

'What was it doing?' she asked.

'Going down along to the stack,' said the rabbit, 'to get a trailer-load of straw bales.'

'My mother's living in the stack,' Flora said.

'Haven't you got no daddy?' the rabbit said.

'He's in the school.'

'They'm separated, huh?'

'Well, yes, they are, just at the moment,' said Flora. 'That's why I'm out here – to fetch my mother and my little sister and take them back to school. They'll be safe there, I hope, and anyway I want them to meet my boyfriend. He's called Buck.'

'Buck?' said the rabbit. 'You got a rabbit for a boyfriend?'

'No, no, he's a mouse. He's ever so handsome. He's pure white, you know, snowy-white, and he's got beautiful pink eyes.'

'And six legs and a pair of dear little wings, I suppose,' said the rabbit. 'I got to hand it to you, mouse. You'm the craziest. I dunno about schoolmouse, seems to me 'tis more fool mouse,' and with these parting words he turned and disappeared down his burrow.

Hyacinth and Love-in-a-mist were unworried at the sound of the tractor's approach. They had grown used to its regular visits to collect a load of straw. What they had not bargained for was that one day, as the stack diminished in size, they might become part of that load.

That morning it so happened that they had made their way to the very edge of the stack, to watch out for Ragged Robin's return, when the tractor driver began to load his trailer.

'Dratted mice!' he said, as he lifted a bale and found two of the creatures hiding beneath it, but before he could do anything, they had leapt on to the bed of the trailer and hidden themselves among the bales already there.

When the tractor returned across the field with its load, Flora had been on the point of leaving the shelter of the rabbit burrow. But hearing it approach, she forced herself to observe it carefully as it went by. It is all part of my education, she told herself, to learn about such things. She noted the features of the great red monster, its driver perched high in his cab, and she ran her eye down the load of straw bales.

Suddenly she saw, right at the bottom of the

load, two anxious faces peeping out between a couple of bales on the bed. One, a small one, she did not recognize. The other she did.

'Mother!' yelled Flora at the top of her voice, and she ran out of the rabbit hole and scuttled along beside the trailer.

'It's our Flora,' said Hyacinth to Love-in-a-mist.

'Jump, Mother! Jump!' cried Flora.

'Jump, Lovey,' said Hyacinth.

'But, Mum . . .' said Love-in-a-mist.

'No buts,' said Hyacinth.

For a mouse, a leap from such a height is the equivalent of a man plunging off the top of a tall building. But mice fall light, and the lush grass cushioned their landing so that they bounced, unhurt.

'Flora!' yelled Hyacinth. 'What are you doing out here?'

'Come to fetch you, Mother,' said Flora.

'But why did your father not come back? I told him to.'

'Is Dad all right?' said Love-in-a-mist.

'You must be Love-in-a-mist,' said Flora. 'You have got a long name, haven't you?'

'Mum usually calls me Lovey.'

'Come on then, Lovey,' said Flora. 'We must all hurry back to school and then I can explain everything.'

'Are you still in the Infants?' asked Hyacinth when they arrived.

'Oh no, Mother,' said Flora. 'I'm a Lower Junior now,' and she led the way to her classroom.

In her absence Ragged Robin and Buck had spent their time in conversation. Buck was feeling guilty at having wounded Flora's father, and Robin was touched at his obvious concern.

'Don't worry, my boy,' he said. 'Least said, soonest mended,' but in fact they said a great deal to one another.

Robin wanted to know all about pet mice and Buck about schoolmice.

'It's this reading business that amazes me, Robin,' he said. 'I don't know how Flora does it. And she can count to thirty-one, and she knows a fantastic lot of things. Education, she calls it. I don't even know what the word means.'

'Me neither, Buck,' said Robin. 'I've been a schoolmouse all my life, but you could count the things I know on the toes of one foot.'

'Talking of feet,' Buck said, 'you should be resting yours. Why not come on down to my place, you'll find it quite comfy.'

So off they went to the Lower Junior classroom, and Robin followed Buck down the hole beneath the sink.

It was indeed a comfortable den, for Buck had pulled a good deal of the lagging off the water pipes, and the two mice took their ease on the most comfortable of thick beds of yellow felt.

The time passed pleasantly as they chatted, and then at last they heard voices above.

'They're here!' said Robin, and he made his way up through the hole in the floorboards and limped, three-legged, towards his wife.

'Hyce, my dear!' he cried. 'You're back!'

Hyacinth regarded her scruffy husband with a stern eye.

'You've been fighting,' she said.

'Well, yes,' said Robin.

'How could you! You are too old for such behaviour.'

'Well, yes,' said Robin.

'You started it, I've no doubt. You went and picked a fight with someone.'

'Well, no,' said Robin.

'And now you've got hurt. Why can't you act your age?'

'But, Hyce . . .' said Robin.

'I'd just like to get hold of the mouse that did it,' said Hyacinth.

'But, Mother . . .' said Flora.

'No buts,' said Hyacinth.

At this point Buck emerged from the hole. He looked, as usual, beautifully groomed, with not a hair out of place. His white coat gleamed, his whiskers were neatly combed.

He lowered the gaze of his pink eyes before Hyacinth's astonished stare.

'I'm sorry,' he said. 'I am the mouse that did it.'

For an instant Hyacinth stood stock-still.

Then she leapt at Buck and fastened her needle-sharp teeth in the end of his nose.

Twelve
In Which Hyacinth Makes an Apology

'Your Bummy,' said Buck that night, 'is a bost fierce bouse.'

Flora licked his swollen snout tenderly.

'I'm sorry,' she said. 'It all happened so quickly. I had no time to explain.'

'She's bade a bess of by dose,' said Buck.

'Lie down and rest,' said Flora, arranging the felt bedding more comfortably around him. 'I expect she'll say she's sorry in her own good time.'

But Hyacinth was in no mood for apologies. That great white monstrosity of a mouse had bitten her poor little husband, so she had responded in kind. 'A nose for a foot and a tooth for a tooth,' she said to Robin, back in their old nest under the staffroom floor.

'You certainly clobbered him, Hyce,' said Robin.

His feelings were muddled. He felt sorry for his new friend, and at the same time pleased that his wife had sprung to avenge his injury.

'You won't do it again though, will you?' he said. 'Now that everything has been explained. I mean, he is one of the family now.'

Hyacinth did not answer.

'I wish I had a boyfriend.' said Lovey.

'You are much too young,' said her mother. 'Why, it seems only yesterday that you were born, here, in this very spot.'

'Buck's place is nice,' said Robin. 'It's much roomier than this and ever so well furnished. Why don't we move in with him and Flora — what d'you say, Hyce?'

But once again Hyacinth did not answer, and Robin knew better than to nag her.

As the next evening approached, only one of the five mice in the school had had a good day's sleep and that was Lovey. Ragged Robin's foot and Buck's nose allowed them no more than a fitful doze, and Flora and Hyacinth were deep in thought.

Each had a problem.

Under the boards in the staffroom Hyacinth now wrestled with her conscience. Should she say she was sorry? She wasn't sorry, but should she say she was? How could they move in with Flora and Buck unless she did say so? What should she do?

Under the sink in the Lower Junior classroom Flora fretted about her future. I shouldn't be here, she said to herself, the summer term will soon be starting and it's time I became a Top Junior. I'm sure I could cope with the work. I want to move up, but I don't want to move house. What shall I do?

As the light faded, Flora's thoughts were interrupted by the sudden appearance of Lovey.

'There's a meeting, Flora,' she said. 'In the staffroom. Now, Mum says,' and away she went.

Flora and Buck made their way to the staffroom, and as soon as they entered, Robin greeted them heartily.

'Flora, dear!' he cried. 'Buck, my boy! How are you feeling?'

'Buch better, thag you, Robid,' said Buck. 'How about you?'

'Oh, I'm on the mend,' said Robin. 'Plenty of life in the old mouse yet.'

An awkward silence followed. Neither of the male mice could think of anything further to say, and Flora's feelings towards her mother were less than kindly. She summoned us here, she thought, so let her get on with it.

After a while Hyacinth spoke.

'Flora,' she said heavily, 'I owe you an apology.'

'Me, Mother?' said Flora, looking sideways at Buck's nose.

'Yes,' said Hyacinth. 'I was hasty. I did not realize that this . . . person . . .'

'Buck,' said Flora. 'His name is Buck.'

'. . . that Buck was a friend of yours.'

'It's not me you should be apologizing to, Mother,' said Flora.

'But . . .' began Hyacinth.

'No buts,' said Flora in so Hyacinth-like a way that Robin was filled with delight. If a mouse could wag its tail like a dog, he'd have wagged his, if he'd had one.

'After all,' said Flora, 'if we are all to live together as one happy family, we don't want any more bad blood.'

'Or any more good blood,' said Robin.

'Well, that was really why I called the meeting,' said Hyacinth hastily, 'to see if you would be willing – you and Buck, that is – for your father and Lovey and me to share your accommodation. It's very comfortable and roomy, I hear, and it would be nice to be all together, wouldn't it?'

'On one condition, Mother,' said Flora firmly.

'What's that?'

'Say you're sorry to Buck.'

'It doesn't batter,' said Buck. 'Least said, soonest bended, eh, Robid?'

Robin did not answer. Go on, Hyce, he thought, say it, even if you don't mean it. It'll do me a power of good to hear you eating humble pie.

Hyacinth looked at the white mouse's still swollen snout. She took a deep breath.

'Buck,' she said, 'I am sorry that I bit your nose,' and to her surprise, she found she meant it.

'Don't bention it,' said Buck.

'Good old Hyce,' said Robin.

'Let's all go to our place,' said Flora.

'Yippee!' cried Lovey, and away they went.

*

The last few
days of the
Easter holidays
slipped by
pleasantly enough.
Both Robin's and Buck's
injuries healed well, and the
white mouse found himself
thoroughly accepted by
Flora's family.

He and Robin were
already firm friends, and
for the little Lovey he was the
perfect big brother. The way to
Hyacinth's heart, he found, was flattery.

Accustomed as she was to nothing better
than such compliments as 'Good old Hyce',

she was delighted
when, for instance,
Buck passed a remark
on the beauty of her
eyes. 'Oh, the depth of

blackness in those shining orbs, Hyacinth,' he murmured, fixing her with his pink ones, and she bridled with pleasure.

Only Flora was restless. As the beginning of the summer term drew near, she haunted the Top Junior classroom. She was determined to move up a class, yet she did not want to leave the comfortable home under the Lower Junior sink.

Then, on the very last day of the holidays, she found the solution. The Top Junior classroom was much the biggest in the school, and one end of it had been set aside as a library area.

Here were not only well-stocked bookshelves, but also a large table on which various books of interest were always left open, to encourage children to look through them. There were atlases and dictionaries and encyclopaedias and many others.

Flora was standing in front of one of these, polishing up her reading skills ready for term time. It was a pictorial dictionary, open at pages dealing with the letter C. The picture was of a man in a suit, carrying a rolled umbrella and a briefcase and in the act of stepping into a railway carriage. It meant nothing to Flora, but she read the words beneath.

C o m m u t e r

One who travels daily from home to place of work, returning home at the end of the day.

That's the way to do it, thought Flora. I don't have to leave home. I can commute to work and back each day.

Thirteen
In Which Flora Has
a Brainwave

Schoolchildren look forward to the holidays and grumble about having to go back to school.

Schoolmice look forward to term time and are less happy when the school is closed and they have the place to themselves. To be sure, it's nice to be able to run about wherever they like, and the peace and quiet is pleasant, but food in holiday time is much harder to come by.

Like all mice, Flora and her family could eat most things, but when there were not children around, their diet was nothing like as varied. They needed to venture outside to gnaw at roots and bulbs, and they ate a great many insects, woodlice in particular being especially crunchy, but the holidays were still a thin time.

For the schoolmice, then, that first day of the summer term was quite a treat. Flora's knowledge of the cleaning ladies' routine meant that she could direct the family to rooms as yet unswept: here they quickly snapped up biscuit crumbs and apple cores and spilled fragments of potato crisps of various flavours (cheese and onion being the favourite) before the arrival of Hoover and broom and dustpan and brush.

That first day in the Top Junior classroom led Flora to another breakthrough. Here there was no handy hole in the wall as in the Infants, no convenient bookshelf as in the Lower Juniors, and already it was plain to her that the library area would be her happiest hunting ground in her search for knowledge.

At lunchtime and in both the morning and afternoon breaks, she came out of hiding and ran busily about the library table, studying the open books.

One of these, the same pictorial dictionary in which she had found 'commuter', had been used that very day and was no longer open at the letter C. The user by chance had been Buck's late owner. Tommy, as usual, was making a nuisance of himself, and the Headmistress had sent him to the library table and told him to sit quietly and look at a book.

Tommy had flicked the pages about aimlessly until he chanced upon a picture that interested him. It was of a cowboy, astride a madly bucking bronco. He went into a daydream in which he defeated all-comers at the rodeo, and he left the book open there.

The word that happened to catch Flora's eye was the one immediately before 'rodeo'.

R o d e n t

it said. Flora read on.

Rodents have distinctive chisel-like
teeth. These teeth grow throughout life
as they are worn away by gnawing.
Common rodents are rats and mice, and

the first warning sign that a building is
infested by them is the discovery of
their droppings. Poison may then be
used against these pests.

Musmors, thought Flora! Don't I know it! And
she remembered poor Sweet William and all the
others who had eaten the dreaded blue pellets.
That's why the people used the poison, she said
to herself, because they found mouse droppings
about the school. They mustn't find ours.

When the commuter arrived home from work,
she told the others what she had read.

'Then we must be careful not to leave our
droppings about in future,' said Hyacinth.

'That's all very well, Hyce,' said Robin, 'but a
mouse has got to do what a mouse has got to do.'

'Perhaps we should use just one place, under
the floorboards?' said Buck.

'It'd get ever so pongy,' said Lovey.

'I'll think of something,' said Flora.

While the others were out foraging (under strict orders not to leave any evidence about), Flora lay in the hole beneath the sink, pondering the problem. She happened to be facing towards the drainpipe, and in her mind's eyes she saw the waste water pouring down inside, carrying away the rinsings of paint pots and brushes and the dirt from childish hands.

Where to, she thought? Where does the gurgling water go?

Bestirring herself, she set out to follow the line of the pipe under-floor. She knew that it took a right-angled turn and went along what was, so to speak, the side wall of their quarters, but she had never explored its course further. Through a sizeable hole in the outer wall of the school it disappeared at last, emerging, Flora found, above a square, brick-built soakaway in which was set a metal grating.

'Perfect!' said Flora. 'The most modern form of sanitation, a water closet, where all will be flushed away. Here shall all our droppings drop.'

And from that day on, they did, each mouse making the short journey to the drainhole whenever he or she felt the call of nature.

'A great idea that, don't you think?' said Buck,

a week or so later, when Flora, having first paid a visit to the soakaway, had commuted to work.

'She's no fool, our Flora,' said Hyacinth.

'It's all this education,' said Ragged Robin. 'I never had none.'

'You never had *any*, Dad,' corrected Lovey.

Robin flared up at this piece of cheek from his younger daughter.

'You keep your trap shut, miss,' he said.

'Robin!' said Hyacinth warningly, for this was bad language among mice, and Lovey moved behind her mother for luck.

But later that evening, when Flora had returned from her classroom and the others were going out and about, Lovey stayed behind for a moment.

'Flora,' she said.

'Yes, Lovey?'

'You're educated, aren't you?'

'Well, not properly. Not yet. I'm getting to know all sorts of things, but there's an awful lot left to learn.'

'Like what?' said Lovey.

'Well,' said Flora, 'like geography and history and science and maybe even French. They had a French lesson today, the Top Juniors did, it was ever so interesting. Do you know what the French for "mouse" is?'

'No,' said Lovey. 'What's French? I don't know anything much. You're lucky, you are,' and she ran off to find the others.

She's right, thought Flora, I *am* lucky. I don't suppose there's another mouse on the face of the earth that knows as much as I do already. And it's only my third term. But I can't talk much about my lessons to the others because they wouldn't understand.

Imagine asking Father to count to 31!

Or asking Mother what's the capital of England.

And my Buck may be handsome, but he doesn't know much more than Lovey does really. They're all uneducated. And why? Because there's no one to teach them.

Thankfully the school was of course empty of people at that moment, because suddenly Flora let out a loud excited squeak.

'Yes, there is!' she cried. 'There's me! I'll start evening classes for them all! I won't be just a schoolmouse. I'll be the world's first ever schoolteachermouse.'

Fourteen
In Which Lovey Plays Truant

Flora's first evening classes were not a great success.

Lovey was keen to learn, certainly. She was curious about things, like Flora, though not as bright.

Buck wanted to be taught, the better to understand some of the subjects that Flora knew so much about. He wished her to be proud of him.

But with Hyacinth and Robin it was a different

matter. They say you shouldn't teach your grandmother to suck eggs, and at first it seemed to Flora that you shouldn't try to teach your parents anything. Hyacinth felt she was being patronized.

'You, teach me?' she said to Flora when she was told of the scheme. 'I could teach you a thing or two, my girl,' but she came along all the same, not wanting to be left behind in the quest for knowledge.

As for Ragged Robin, he was willing, but dim. He feared very much that he would be the dunce and that the others would look down on him.

The lessons took place in the Infant classroom.

Since Flora's days as an Infant, the teacher had put up on the wall a large picture alphabet, the writing on it so big as to be clearly visible even to Buck's poor eyesight.

'I have brought you here,' said Flora, confronting her class of three schoolmice and one pet mouse, 'because the first and most important thing, for mice or humans, is to learn to read. Once you can do that, there is no limit to what you can get into your heads.'

Robin shook his, doubtfully.

'And before you can learn to read,' went on Flora, 'you must learn your alphabet. There it is. Now then, the first letter of the alphabet is A.'

'A what?' said Hyacinth.

'Just listen, please, Mother,' said Flora, 'and don't interrupt. The second letter is B.'

'A bee!' said Robin in a pleased voice. 'I've seen them! Nearly got stung once.'

'No, no,' said Flora. 'Just wait, Father, you don't understand.'

'I knew I wouldn't,' said Robin dolefully.

'And the third letter of the alphabet is C.'

'See,' said Buck. 'Yes, I see.'

'I don't,' said Lovey. 'I'm muddled. Start again, Flora.'

That first lesson was hard going for everyone, but then Flora devised a way of teaching them the alphabet that was more fun. She invented a rhyme, and made them learn it by heart. It went like this.

A B C D E F G
Oh what clever mice are we!
H I J K L M N

Mice are just as bright as men.

O P Q R ST U

And to prove that this is true

V and **W X Y Z**

That's the alphabet we've read!

Thanks to this method, Flora's class more or less mastered their A B C , though Robin was sometimes apt to get his tongue in a twist. Now they could actually begin to learn to read.

For Flora, that summer term was a hard slog. By day she educated herself, and in the evenings she taught her class. But she had not the advantages of the human teacher. She could not select the proper books from the shelves. Turning the pages of those she found lying about was not at all easy, and, of course, she could not make use of the blackboard.

But gradually, as time passed, her pupils began to recognize some common words and Lovey in particular was making quite good progress. She can almost read, said Flora to herself, but I'm not so sure about the others. There's a lot of guessing going on. I ought to test them. On a very simple book of course.

And that, by chance, was what she found.

Though the school itself was very old, most of the books in the Infant classroom were quite modern. But one or two remained that must have been there from the beginning.

Flora found just such a one when nosing around the shelves. She cocked her head sideways to read the title on the spine.

MY VERY FIRST READING BOOK

it said.

Excellent, thought Flora, it shall be theirs.

By pushing and pulling at it, the five of them managed to dislodge it from the shelf, and it fell on the floor, open.

'Ah!' cried Flora. 'What luck! There are several short simple sentences on these pages. Now I want you all to study them carefully –

there are no pictures here to help you —
and then I shall ask each of you in turn to
read a sentence out loud to the rest of the
class. It will be your very first test, to see
how well you can read. Mother, will you
read the top line, please?'

Hyacinth studied the first line.

'See the boy play with his kite.'

She recognized the word 'boy', which she had often come across.

'It's about a boy,' she said.

'Yes, good,' said Flora. 'What is the boy doing?'

'Give me a hint,' said Hyacinth.

'Something up in the sky,' said Flora.

'The boy is flying,' said Hyacinth hopefully.

'Yes, well, good try, Mother,' said Flora, and she read the sentence correctly.

'Flying his kite,' said Hyacinth. 'Yes, that's what I was going to say.'

'Now, Father,' said Flora. 'Try the next line.'

Robin looked nervously at the second sentence.

'Meg has a nice new doll.'

He recognized the word 'a', but the rest was a mystery. I bet it's one of those ones we learned, he thought.

' "Mice are just as bright as men",' he said.

'Not quite,' said Flora. 'Buck, can you read it?'

'Not really,' said Buck. 'The print is so small. My eyesight, you know.'

So Flora read that one out, and then asked Lovey to try the third sentence, which was

'The cat sat on the mat.'

And slowly, but quite correctly, Lovey read it!

'Wonderful!' cried Flora. 'Good girl, Lovey!'

'That can't be right,' said Robin grumpily. 'I'm sure it should be

"The cat sat on the rat."

Anyone can see that makes much more sense.'

Flora kept on with *My Very First Reading Book* for

the remainder of the summer term. Each evening the mice pulled it down and each morning the Infant teacher, much surprised, put it back into the shelves. She tried to find out which child was responsible, but 'Not me, miss!' was all she got.

She would have been even more surprised could she have seen what went on one warm July evening towards the end of term. Flora had been taking a nap in the family home after her day's studies. She told the others she would meet them in the Infant classroom later.

She woke and stretched, thinking that perhaps she would try a little number work with the class. Here there was a calendar too. The calendar hung on the wall as usual, and Lovey at least, she felt sure, would soon get the hang of it.

When she arrived, it was to find that *My Very First Reading Book* had already been pulled down, and she was just in time to hear Buck say, very slowly, with long pauses between words,

'Spot is good. Good dog, Spot.'

'Buck!' she cried. 'That was brilliant! You'll be catching up with Lovey at this rate.'

Hyacinth looked round.

'Where is Lovey?' she said.

'Don't know,' said Robin.

'I saw her not long ago,' said Buck.

'Lovey!' they all squeaked.

But there was no answer, so they searched the school, calling and calling and looking everywhere.

But Lovey was gone.

Fifteen
In Which All Ends Happily

Term ended. The children and the teachers went home. The cleaning ladies cleaned up. The caretaker locked up. Once more the schoolmice had the school to themselves. But now there were only four of them. Buck felt sad. Because she was small for her age and, of course, because she was Flora's sister, he had grown fond of Lovey and her cheeky ways.

Ragged Robin was ill-tempered.

'Life's not fair,' he said to Flora. 'Why do all these misfortunes happen to us?'

'Come and read to me, Father,' said Flora. 'It'll take your mind off things.'

'Read?' said Robin. 'Certainly not. I have broken up for the summer holidays.'

Hyacinth seemed less worried than the others. She went about in a preoccupied manner, and was choosy about her food, developing a sudden addiction to soap, which she nibbled at in the sink.

Flora thought hard about Lovey's chances of survival. They're not good, she said to herself. Why she went, I've no idea, but she'll live to regret it. Or rather she won't live.

A French phrase book chanced to be lying open on the library table, and as Flora was studying it, she saw something that seemed to sum up the situation.

Adieu – farewell, good wishes at a final parting
Au revoir – goodbye until we meet again.

But I'm afraid we shan't meet again, thought Flora. *Adieu*, Lovey. Later that day she was alone with Buck.

'Well,' she said, 'it looks like the end of my evening classes for the moment. Lovey's gone, Father flatly refuses to come, and Mother says she's too busy, though I can't see it myself. That only leaves you.'

'A class of one,' said Buck.

'Yes.'

'That means you could devote yourself to me. If you were willing.'

Oh Buck, thought Flora, I am devoted to you, you great white handsome beast!

'Of course I'm willing,' she said. 'I'd do anything for you, you know that.'

Buck's pink eyes seemed to turn even redder.

'Oh Flora!' he breathed, and their whiskers mixed as they touched noses.

The weather was very hot, even at nights, and since there was no need for caution, the schoolmice relaxed wherever they fancied, always remembering, of course, to return to the brick-built soakaway whenever nature called.

Only Hyacinth remained in the hole under the sink in the Lower Junior classroom, in so tetchy a mood that Robin took himself off to the old staffroom den for a bit of peace and quiet.

As for Flora and Buck, they decided to make use of the hole in the wall over the teacher's desk in the Infant classroom. It was cool and airy, and handy for the schoolteachermouse and her solitary pupil.

About halfway through the holidays, they were sitting together on the desk, bathed in a glow of contentment. Both teacher and pupil had good reason to be happy, for Buck, with his back turned to the calendar on the wall, had just succeeded in counting to 31.

'I must tell Mother!' Flora said. 'Don't move. Have a rest. You've earned it.'

'Mother!' she called down the hole under the sink. 'What do you think? Buck can count to thirty-one.'

'Six is all I can manage,' replied Hyacinth. 'Come and have a look.'

'Oh, Mother!' cried Flora when she saw the

half-dozen newborn babies, fat and pink and naked and hideous. 'They're beautiful!'

'Fetch your father,' said Hyacinth. 'He's in the staffroom.'

Ragged Robin was not best pleased at being summoned.

'Now what have I done wrong?' he said to Flora.

'Nothing wrong, Father,' said Flora. 'It's a nice surprise.'

And to Robin, it was.

'Hyce!' he cried when he saw his third crop of sons and daughters. 'You never told me! I never knew!'

'Well, now you do,' said Hyacinth shortly.

A horrid thought occurred to Robin, whose knowledge of heredity was sketchy.

'Have they all got tails?' he asked.

'Poor Father,' said Flora to Buck later in the hole in the wall. 'He always says the wrong things and then Mother gets furious with him.'

'I'm glad you don't get furious with me,' said Buck.

'You always say the right things,' said Flora.

'Flora!' said Buck fondly, and immediately the word seemed to echo through the school — 'Flora! Flora! Flora!'

But the echo was more high-pitched and the tone of it was familiar.

'It's Lovey!' cried Flora, and she ran down to the floor, Buck following. 'In here, Lovey!' she called. 'We're in the Infants!'

In a moment the small figure of Lovey appeared in the doorway.

'I'm back!' she said. 'Wait there. I'll fetch my friend.'

'I didn't know you had a friend,' said Flora.

'I didn't,' said Lovey, 'but I have now. I'll just go and get him. He's a bit shy.'

Flora and Buck looked at one another, but before they could speak, Lovey returned. Following her, rather reluctantly, was an even smaller mouse.

'This is Haycorn,'
said Lovey. 'Haycorn, this
is my sister Flora and her boyfriend Buck.'

Haycorn took one look at Buck and turned
tail, ready to flee, but Lovey reassured him.

'It's all right,' she said. 'Buck's ever so nice.
He's just white, that's all, he can't help it.'

'Lovey,' said Flora. 'We've all been worried
stiff. Wherever have you been all this time?'

'I've been down at the farm,' said Lovey.
'There's Mum and Dad, and there's you and
Buck, and I said to myself, Come along, Love-in-

a-mist, my girl, it's time you started living up to your name. So I went down to the farm on a nice misty evening, and who should I meet but Haycorn. He's a farm mouse, you see, but I've been telling him he'll like it up here.'

'I'm sure he will,' said Flora and Buck with one voice.

'You will, won't you, Haycorn?' said Lovey.

'Yes, Lovey,' said the very small mouse in a very small voice.

'And you'll come to Flora's class with us and learn to read.'

'Yes, Lovey,' said Haycorn.

'He may not want to,' said Flora.

'He will,' said Lovey. 'Come along now, Haycorn. I'll introduce you to Mum and Dad.'

'Oh, by the way,' said Flora. 'Mother's had six more babies.'

'Oh goody!' cried Lovey. 'I adore babies. I just can't wait.'

'Wait for what, Lovey?' said Haycorn.

Lovey gave a squeak of amusement.

'He's very young,' she said to Flora, 'but he'll learn,' and off she dashed, followed by her little swain.

'Fancy!' said Flora. 'You have to admire her, Buck. Off she goes without telling a soul, finds her way to the farm, and picks up a boyfriend.'

'She practically could pick him up,' said Buck, 'he's so small. Not much more than a baby really. And talking of babies, I haven't seen these new ones yet.'

'Do you want to?' said Flora.

'Oh yes. Lovey's not the only one who's fond of babies. I just wish . . .' and then he stopped.

'Just wish what, Buck?' said Flora.

'Oh nothing,' said Buck.

He sighed.

'You've got your career,' he said.

'Yes, indeed,' said Flora. 'What with you and Mother and Father and Lovey and Haycorn and before long Mother's new six, I shall have a big class to teach, a class of . . . well, you do the sum, Buck. How many?'

'Eleven,' said Buck.

'Well done,' said Flora. 'You may have started life as a pet mouse, but you're learning fast. I'm proud of you. Your reading especially is coming on a treat. Which reminds me, I remember finding something in *My Very First Reading Book* that I want to show you now. Help me get it off the shelf.'

When the book had fallen to the ground, Flora began to turn the pages with her nose, looking at each until she found the one she wanted.

'Ah yes, here it is,' she said at last. 'Read me this sentence, will you, Buck, the one I've got my paw on?'

'Children are a great blessing.'

read Buck, with a little help from his teacher.

'Would you agree?' said Flora.

Buck stared at her across the pages of *My Very First Reading Book*.

'You mean . . .?' he said softly.

'I mean,' said Flora, 'that we are to be blessed. Shortly before the start of the Christmas term, I reckon.'

'Oh, Flora!' said Buck. 'How marvellous! And what extraordinary children they will be, with your brains' (and your beauty, thought Flora) 'and with you to teach them. Why, there will be no limit to their scholarship. Oh, Flora, you have made me the happiest white mouse in the world.'

'And you,' said Flora, 'have made me the happiest schoolmouse.'